First published 2014 by Macmillan Children's Books, a division of Macmillan Publishers Limited

20 New Wharf Road, London N1 9RR, Basingstoke and Oxford

Associated companies throughout the world

1 3 5 7 9 8 6 4 2

ISBN: 978-0-230-74250-5

Text and illustrations © Catherine Rayner 2014

Moral rights asserted.

www.panmacmillan.com

A CIP catalogue record for this book is available from the British Library.

Printed in China

For
Florence
x

SMELLY
LOUIE

Catherine Rayner

Macmillan Children's Books

Louie had just had a bath.

He smelt of roses and apple blossom,
and he was NOT happy about it!

Something was missing.
His own Special Smell had gone . . .

and he wanted it back.

Louie trotted out into the
garden where he found a fox.

The fox smelt, A LOT.

"Where did you find
YOUR smell?"
asked Louie.

"Well, it's been building up for years," explained the fox. "But there is something over in the brambles that might be worth a sniff."

Louie followed his nose and found . . .

an OLD BOOT!

The boot smelt good, like mouldy cheese.
But something was still missing.

Some nearby snails suggested he search
in the alleyway. Louie followed his nose
and found . . .

STINKY BINS!

They were overflowing with fishy leftovers,
and cabbage leaves mixed with rotten eggs.

Delicious! But it was
still not his own
Special Smell.

Some friendly flies were lingering and they knew of something wonderfully whiffy just down the road . . .

STICKY SLUDGE!

Louie wriggled and rolled.
His smell was getting better.
But it still needed
something else.

Then he remembered . . .

the PONGY POND!

Louie wallowed and splashed.
His Special Smell was back,
and it was AMAZING!

Louie had had a very good day.
Everything had worked out beautifully!

He trotted happily back home
with his Special Smell wafting
all around him.

The fox was VERY impressed.

Louie sauntered into the house and up the stairs.

And that was when he heard The Noise . . .

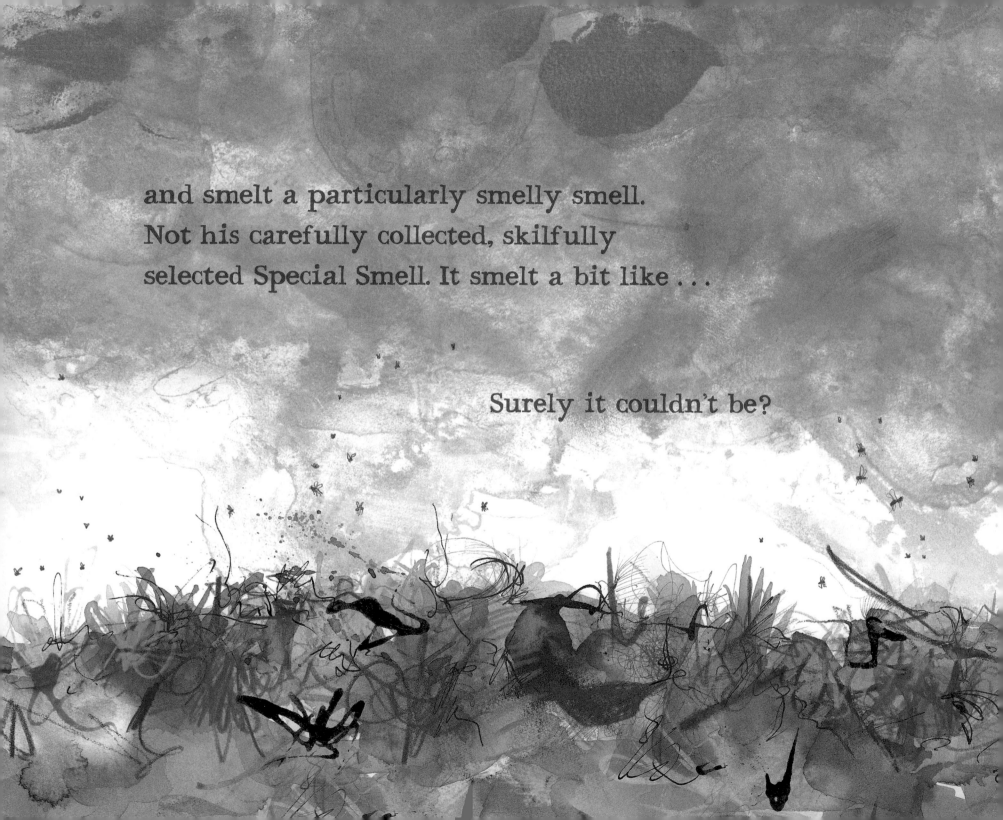

and smelt a particularly smelly smell.
Not his carefully collected, skilfully
selected Special Smell. It smelt a bit like . . .

Surely it couldn't be?

Roses and apple blossom!

Oh no!

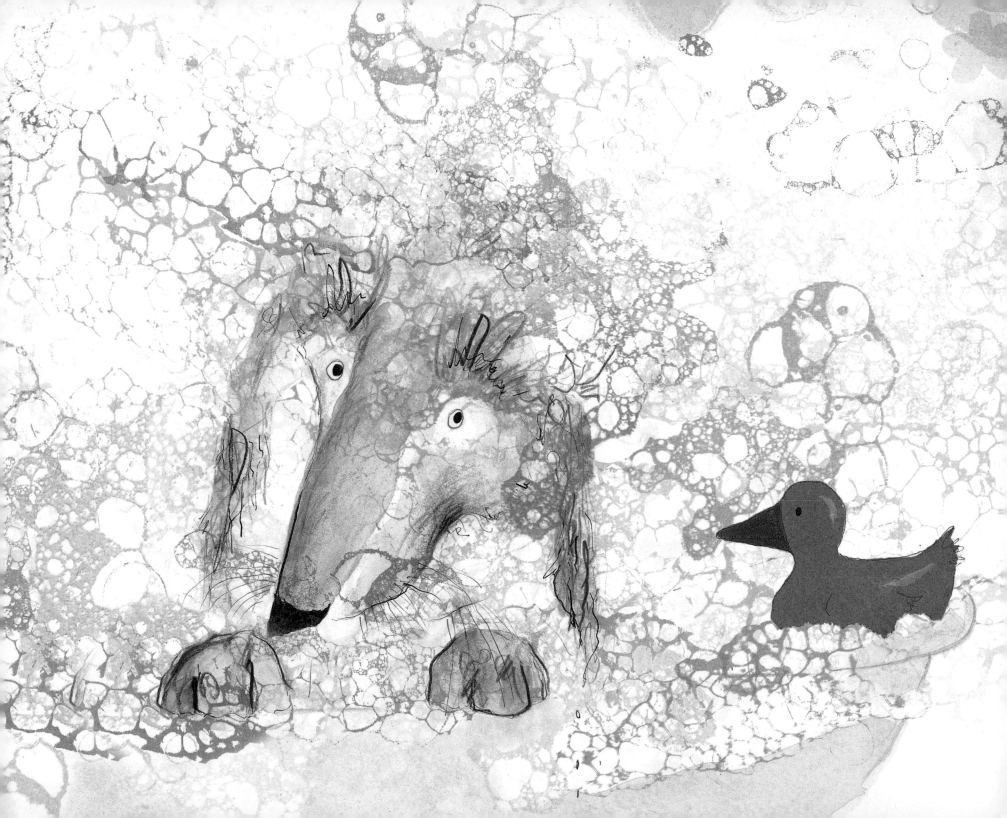